A Book of
PRINCESSES

SALLY GARDNER

Orion
Children's Books

To my mum
Nina Lowry
for all her love and support

First published in Great Britain in 1997
by Orion Children's Books
a division of the Orion Publishing Group Ltd
Orion House
5 Upper St Martin's Lane
London WC2H 9EA

Copyright © Sally Gardner 1997
Designed by Ian Butterworth

The right of Sally Gardner to be identified as the author and illusrator of
this work has been asserted.

A catalogue record for this book is available from the British Library

Printed in Italy
ISBN 1 85881 350 6

CONTENTS

C I N D E

R E L L A

ONCE UPON A TIME THERE LIVED A BEAUTIFUL GIRL CALLED CINDERELLA. Cinderella was not her real name, but that was what her stepmother and two stepsisters called her after her father had remarried.

When Cinderella's mother died, her father was heartbroken, and didn't know what to do for the best. Then he met a lady with two daughters of Cinderella's age, who seemed to be just what he needed. She was keen to be his wife, and in no time at all they were married.

Now surely nothing could be more perfect. Cinderella would have a kind stepmother to look after her, and two sweet stepsisters as well.

BUT OH DEAR ME, HOW WRONG HE WAS! For as soon as the wedding was over, Cinderella was moved out of her bedroom and down to the kitchen, where she was to live and work as a servant. Cinderella's father begged his new wife to change her mind, but he soon realized he had made a terrible mistake. She was a jealous woman with a wicked temper.

Cinderella's stepsisters, Henrietta and Georgina, were spoilt, unattractive girls who took great delight in bullying Cinderella. Their doting mother was determined that one of her daughters should marry a prince, so she spent a small fortune on lessons in talking nicely, walking nicely, and smiling nicely. She gave them whatever they wanted,

but nothing made the two sisters any happier or kinder. In fact, the more they were given, the meaner and nastier they became.

Nobody took any notice of Cinderella. She just did the housework. She did everything she was told to without complaining, but she did think it was unfair.

Her father could do nothing for her. He was much too frightened of his new wife.

Time went on and nothing changed. Much to the fury of her stepmother and stepsisters, Cinderella grew up to be beautiful and kind. Her stepsisters, for all their fine clothes, lacked any beauty or grace. This was a pity, because their mother had great plans for them.

ONE DAY THE KING ANNOUNCED
THAT HE WAS GIVING A VERY
GRAND BALL.

All the unmarried ladies in the land
were to be invited, so that his son the prince
could choose a bride.

When the invitation arrived,
Cinderella's stepmother saw that this was
the moment she had been waiting for.

"Henrietta, my darling! Georgina,
my precious!" she cried. "Wonderful
news! You're both invited to the ball.
The prince is bound to fall for one of
you girls. What a wedding
it will be!"

"But Mama, we haven't
a thing to wear!" screeched
Georgina and Henrietta.

So Cinderella's father had to pay for still more fine dresses and shoes for his stepdaughters. He was at his wits' end. Cinderella was made to work even harder. There were no end of extra jobs for her to do.

At last the day of the ball arrived, and Cinderella helped her stepsisters to get ready. How she longed to put on a lovely dress and go with them to the ball! Georgina and Henrietta knew this and enjoyed teasing her.

"Don't you wish you could come to the ball too, Cinderella?" said Georgina.

"Don't be silly," said Henrietta. "Can you see anyone dancing with Cinderella dressed in those rags?"

Cinderella said nothing. She finished her work, helped her father, stepmother and two stepsisters into their carriage, and waved them off to the ball. Then she went back to the cold kitchen, sat down by the fire and wept. She was so very, very unhappy.

WIPING THE TEARS FROM HER EYES, SHE WAS SURPRISED TO SEE A LADY STANDING BESIDE HER.

"Oh dear me, tears down such a lovely face!" said the lady.

"Who are you?" asked Cinderella.

"Your fairy godmother," said the lady. "I am supposed to come when you really need me. I must say, it has been very difficult. You have needed me so much and I am only allowed one visit. This royal ball is just the ticket."

"Oh, I'm so glad you came! I did so wish I could go to the ball," said Cinderella, "but it's too late now, and anyway, I've nothing to wear. My sisters would be furious if I even touched one of their dresses."

"Stuff and nonsense!" said her fairy godmother. "We don't want borrowed clothes or carriages! Now, let's see what we have here."

She waved her magic wand, and there in front of Cinderella were four beautifully wrapped boxes. Cinderella opened each box with great excitement. It was years since she had been given a present. But what strange presents they were! A pumpkin, six white mice, three fat rats and four lizards.

"Thank you," said Cinderella, a little puzzled. "I am sure they will make lovely pets, and the pumpkin will make a delicious pie."

"PETS AND PIES MY FOOT!" SAID HER FAIRY GODMOTHER.
"Come into the garden. I've something to show you."

Cinderella followed her out of the kitchen. Her fairy godmother waved her wand over the pumpkin, and there stood a golden carriage. She waved her wand again and the six white mice became horses, the three fat rats were

turned into handsome coachmen and the four lizards into footmen dressed in scarlet.

"How wonderful!" cried Cinderella, clapping her hands with joy.

"Well, my dear, your carriage awaits to take you to the ball."

"I don't mean to sound ungrateful," said Cinderella, "but surely I can't go dressed like this?"

"Oh silly me," said her fairy godmother.
"I nearly forgot the best part." She waved her
wand, and Cinderella found herself wearing the
most beautiful dress, with a pair of sparkling
shoes made of glass on her feet.

CINDERELLA STEPPED INTO THE CARRIAGE. "Just one thing before you go," said her fairy godmother. "You must promise me that you will leave the ball before the clock strikes midnight. If you don't, all my magic will vanish. Don't forget, you have got to leave before midnight strikes. REMEMBER, BEFORE MIDNIGHT STRIKES."

Meanwhile, at the palace Henrietta and Georgina and all the other fine ladies were introduced to the charming young prince. But oh dear! oh dear! They all looked the same to him. The prince didn't want to marry any of them.

Then a trumpet sounded, Cinderella entered the room and the prince's heart went BOOM. Everybody stopped what they were doing and turned to look at her.

THE PRINCE DANCED WITH CINDERELLA FOR
THE WHOLE EVENING.

IT WAS MAGIC.

"It's very rude of him," said Georgina, sulking. "Fancy only dancing with her, whoever she is."

"If I was wearing that dress I know the prince would want to dance with me," said Henrietta.

"She isn't half as pretty as either of you," said their mother.

The prince was head over heels in love with Cinderella. She was as sweet and kind as she looked, and he knew that he loved her with all his heart.

All too soon the clock struck a quarter to twelve. Cinderella could hardly believe it was so late.

"Oh dear, look at the time! I'll have to go! Thank you, thank you for a lovely evening!" she cried.

"Don't go! Just one more dance!" pleaded the prince.

"Well, just one more," said Cinderella.

Cinderella was so happy she could have danced until morning. But to her dismay she heard the clock begin to strike the hour ...

"I'll be late! I really must go," said Cinderella.

"Please stay," said the prince. "I want to ask you to …"

ONE … TWO …

But it was too late. Cinderella was already running out of the ballroom.

THREE … FOUR …

As she ran, she lost one of her glass shoes. She had no time to turn back, so she took off the other shoe …

FIVE … SIX …

ran to the carriage and jumped in. The coachman cracked his whip and the carriage sped away …

SEVEN … EIGHT …

past the palace guards …

NINE … TEN …

and out of the palace gates …

ELEVEN …

just before the last note sounded …

TWELVE …

21

m i d n

CINDERELLA FOUND HERSELF STANDING ALL ALONE IN THE KITCHEN IN HER OLD RAGS.

Perhaps it was a dream? But then she looked down and saw that she was still holding one glass shoe. She quickly put it in her pocket.

A FEW MINUTES LATER HER STEPMOTHER AND STEPSISTERS CAME STOMPING INTO THE HOUSE. They were all in a terrible mood.

"What a waste of time!" said Georgina, throwing her cloak and gloves on the floor. "That girl spoiled everything! It's not fair."

"I'd be as beautiful as her if I had a dress like that," said Henrietta.

"I tell you this, my precious girls, it won't do the prince any good falling in love with her, whoever she is," said Cinderella's stepmother. "All that's left of her is a glass shoe."

"He can't marry a shoe!" said Henrietta.

"Where's Cinderella?" they all shouted together. "We're hungry, we want some tea. Tidy up this mess, you lazy girl!"

And Cinderella came running to do what they wanted.

The very next day the prince announced that he would marry the lady whose tiny foot fitted the glass shoe, and that he would search the whole kingdom until he found her.

Cinderella heard this with a sad heart, for she had fallen in love with the prince. But what hope had she of ever seeing him again?

Henrietta and Georgina had their feet massaged daily and drank nothing but rose water. Each hoped that her rather large foot would fit the glass shoe.

One day there was a knock at the door and the prince walked in, followed by a footman carrying the now famous tiny glass shoe.

"Me first," said Henrietta, pushing Georgina out of the way.

"No, me!" said Georgina, kicking Henrietta.

"Ladies! One at a time please!" said the footman.

GEORGINA WENT FIRST. SHE TRIED HER HARDEST TO SQUEEZE HER FOOT INTO THE DAINTY SHOE.

She tried once, she tried twice, she tried three times before finally giving up.

Henrietta did no better. There was no way her big foot would ever fit the magical shoe.

"Oh bother!" said Henrietta.

"Oh blast!" said Georgina.

"Oh thank goodness!" said the prince.

The prince was feeling low. He had visited every house where a young lady was living, and he had not found his love. He was just about to leave when Cinderella's father spoke up. He was usually too frightened to say boo to a goose.

"I have a daughter, sir, who hasn't yet tried on the shoe," he said.

"Please be kind enough to bring her here," said the prince.

" You don't need to see her, sir, she's a stupid good-for-nothing girl," said Cinderella's stepmother.

"But I would like to see her, just the same," said the prince.

Cinderella walked into the room. The prince saw a beautiful girl dressed in rags, and knew at once that this was his princess. He gently placed the glass shoe on her foot. It was a perfect fit.

"Impossible!" said her stepmother.

"It must be a mistake!" screamed Georgina.

"She's tricking you!" yelled Henrietta.

CINDERELLA TOOK THE OTHER GLASS SHOE FROM THE POCKET OF HER APRON, AND AT THAT MOMENT HER FAIRY GODMOTHER ARRIVED.

With a wave of her magic wand she changed Cinderella into a beautiful princess.

"Oh, I wouldn't have missed this for all the tea in China," said the fairy godmother. "It has all turned out so well."

The prince took Cinderella back to his palace. A week later they were married, and they lived happily ever after.

FOOTNOTE:

Cinderella's stepmother and stepsisters were not popular after the news spread about how badly they had treated Cinderella. I did hear that the two stepsisters were later married to noblemen. I just hope their husbands were happy.

As for Cinderella's father, the king invited him to live in the palace so he could be near his daughter, and this suited him very well indeed.

THE FRO

ONCE UPON A TIME THERE LIVED A GOOD
AND WISE KING. HE HAD SEVEN
BEAUTIFUL DAUGHTERS AND HE LOVED THEM
ALL VERY MUCH.

One sunny afternoon the youngest
princess had nothing much to do,
so she went for a walk in the
woods. She sat down beside a
stream and began to play with
her favourite toy, a little
golden ball.

She threw it high into the air. She loved to see

G PRINCE

But she threw it
too high and it fell
into the stream with a splash.
The princess leaned over the water's edge
as far as she dared, trying to get it back,
but it was hopeless. She started to cry.

"I would give anything in the world
to have my darling ball back again," she
said aloud.

Just then a frog poked his head out of
the water. "CROAK! I can get your ball
back," he said. "All I want in return is
the promise that I can eat from your
plate and sleep on your bed, and
that in the morning you will give
me a kiss."

"OH, HOW VERY SILLY THIS FROG IS," thought the princess. "What use is a promise to him? He will never be able to leave this stream."

So, feeling very pleased that it would cost her so little to get her ball back, she said, "If you bring me back my golden ball I will promise all you ask."

The frog dived down into the stream and after a while came up with the ball in his mouth and dropped it on the ground. The princess was thrilled. She picked up the ball and ran home, forgetting all about the frog and the promise she had made.

That evening the king held a party for his seven daughters. He had invited seven charming princes to keep them company. They had just sat down to eat when there was a gentle knock at the door, and a soft voice called the king's youngest daughter. The princess ran to the door and opened it. There, to her horror, sat the frog.

"CROOAAK!"

THE PRINCESS FELT TERRIBLY FRIGHTENED.
She shut the door quickly and went back
to her chair.

"What's the matter, my sweet?" asked the
king. "You look pale."

So the princess told him what the frog had
said. Everybody thought it was very funny.
Everybody, that is, except the king, who was
very cross.

"You made a foolish promise," said the
king, "and now you must keep it." He asked
the frog to come and sit on the table next to
the princess's plate. The frog thanked the king
and began to eat.

The whole party watched with disgust as
the princess shared her food with the frog. At
the end of the meal the frog said he was tired
and ready for bed. The princess could not
bring herself to touch him,
so she carried the frog
upstairs on her empty plate
and put him down in the
corner of her room.

"You can sleep here," said the princess.

"No," said the frog. "I must sleep on your bed as you promised."

So the princess put the frog on her pillow and cried herself to sleep.

In the morning nothing would make her kiss the frog. He didn't seem to mind. He hopped away into the palace grounds.

"Thank goodness that's over. I will never see that ugly frog again," said the princess.
BUT SHE WAS WRONG.

"CROOAAAK!"

That night the frog came back, and again he ate from the princess's plate and slept on her pillow.

In the morning he waited to be kissed, but the princess couldn't bring herself to do it. The frog seemed to be growing uglier by the minute.

"CROOAAAAK!"

On the third night the frog was back again. For the third time he ate from the princess's plate and lay on her pillow. But tonight as he lay there the frog told a story of such magic and enchantment that the princess fell into a deep and peaceful sleep, in which she dreamed that she had married a prince as handsome as the moon and as bright as the stars.

IN THE MORNING WHEN SHE WOKE, THE PRINCESS DECIDED TO GET THE KISS OVER AND DONE WITH.

The frog tilted his head for the kiss. The princess, who thought this was going to be really horrid, like taking the most disgusting medicine, kissed the frog. And suddenly – the frog was gone, and the prince from her dreams stood before her!

BEAUTY

Like all proud parents they wanted the very best for their baby, so they invited the seven good fairies of the kingdom to be godmothers. Seven invitations were written but only six handed out, for the seventh fairy could not be found. She had fallen out with her sisters, locked herself away in a tower, and turned her good magic into bad. When the king heard this, he tore up her invitation.

THE GREAT DAY ARRIVED AND THE CASTLE WAS PACKED WITH PEOPLE WHO HAD COME TO THE PARTY. The six good fairies were the guests of honour. One by one they gave their presents to the baby princess:

HAPPINESS,

BEAUTY,

WISDOM,

LAUGHTER,

AND A VOICE LIKE AN ANGEL.

The sixth fairy was just about to give her
present when the doors of the great hall burst
open. There stood the seventh fairy, face as
cold as frost, eyes as bright as fire. She came
near to the cradle. The queen picked up her
sleeping baby and held her tight. The seventh
fairy pointed a finger as sharp as a knife.

"I HAVE A PRESENT FOR YOUR PRECIOUS BABY," SHE SAID. "DON'T YOU WANT TO KNOW WHAT IT IS?"

"No!" said the king. "Go away and leave us in peace."

The seventh fairy stamped her foot. The castle rumbled.

"You should have invited me to the christening," she said. "You will regret this." She turned and looked at the other fairies. "So, my goody goody sisters, what magical presents did you give the baby?"

"Will you please leave!" said the king.

"Leave! Leave!" yelled the seventh fairy. "I haven't given my present yet! Since this is the way you treat me, here is my gift. When this baby girl is sixteen years old she will prick her finger on a spindle and she will

die!"

"Arrest this woman!" shouted the king. Soldiers charged in, but the seventh fairy had vanished.

The queen cried, and everybody was very upset. Then the sixth fairy spoke.

"I didn't get the chance to give the princess my present. I cannot undo all that my wicked sister has done, but I can make sure the princess will not die. Instead she will fall asleep for a hundred years, until she is woken with a kiss from a prince."

"Why a hundred years?" wept the queen. But all the good fairies would say is that if the seventh fairy's curse came about, they were to be sent for.

F ROM THAT DAY ALL SPINNING WHEELS
WERE BANNED FROM THE CASTLE AND
THE WHOLE KINGDOM. The princess grew up
to have all the things the good fairies had
promised. She was beautiful, wise, full of
laughter and happiness, with a voice like an
angel. She knew nothing about the seventh
fairy's present.

When the princess was sixteen,
the king and queen gave a birthday
party for her. As always with parties,
there was a lot to be done. No one
wanted the birthday girl to get in their
way, so the princess passed the time
wandering about the castle playing
with her little dog. Near her old
playroom she saw a door she had
never noticed before.

"That's strange," said the princess, opening the door, "I thought I knew every corner of the castle." She walked up some winding stairs that led up into a tower, where a wizened old woman sat at a spinning wheel.

"Don't be frightened, my beauty," said the old woman, holding out a hand with fingers as sharp as knives. "I have waited sixteen years to show you how to spin."

47

The princess went closer, for she had never seen a spinning wheel before. She sat down to spin. At once, **she** pricked her finger and fell to the floor, fast asleep.

The seventh fairy vanished, but her words rang out around the castle.

"THE PRINCESS IS

48

SIXTEEN AND I HAVE GIVEN HER MY PRESENT!"

THE KING BROUGHT HIS DAUGHTER DOWN FROM THE TOWER AND LAID HER UPON A BED WITH COVERS EMBROIDERED IN SILVER AND GOLD.

The six good fairies were sent for. They soon arrived and went about their work with great care, for they could see into the future and they did not want the princess to wake up alone.

Soon the castle and everything in it lay in an enchanted sleep. The horses in the stable,

the cat chasing the mouse, the food on the plates, the fire in the grate – nothing escaped the magic wand of sleep. To keep them all safe until the hundred years were over, a forest of thorns sprang up around the castle, so thick and dense that neither friend nor foe could get through.

IN TIME THE CASTLE AND THE SLEEPING PRINCESS WERE NO MORE REAL THAN A STORY TOLD TO CHILDREN.

A hundred years later a prince from a neighbouring kingdom was out hunting. He came to the edge of the forest of thorns, and wondered what lay behind it. Giants? Goblins? Dragons?

Then he remembered his mother telling him a story of a castle in the heart of this forest, where a princess slept whose beauty was given to her by the fairies. Her sleep would last for a hundred years, until she was woken by a kiss from a prince.

As the prince stood there, the hedge of thorns parted and a path appeared before him. He walked straight through, and the wall of thorns closed in behind him.

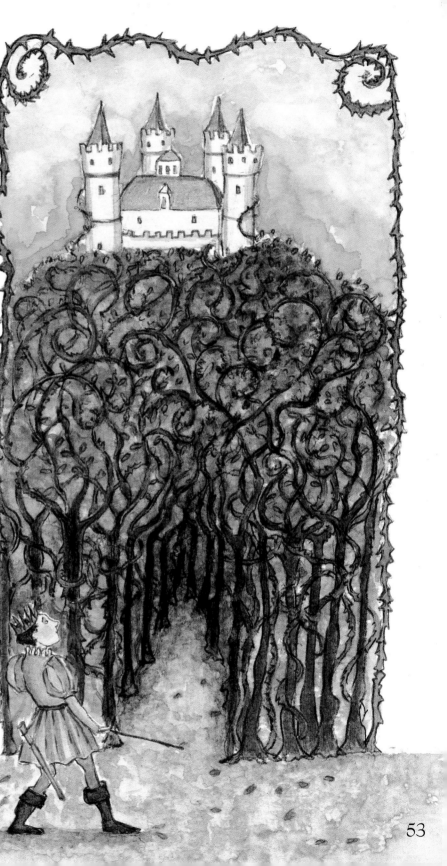

THE SILENCE OF A HUNDRED YEARS LAY OVER THE FOREST. NO BIRDS SANG. But the prince bravely went on until he came to the castle, its walls covered in brambles as sharp as knives.

He stepped over the sleeping guards, climbed up the steps, and pushed open the heavy castle door.

It was just like the story. Everything lay in an enchanted sleep. The prince wandered through room after room. He saw the cook icing the birthday cake, a page boy stealing a chocolate, a footman kissing a maid, a dog about to trip up the butler, the butler carrying a tray of glasses, and lots of lords and ladies putting on their finery. All of them had fallen asleep just where they were.

54

At last he came to the room where the
sleeping princess lay. Never before had he seen
such a beautiful girl. She had lips as red as
roses, and skin as soft as petals. He leant over
and gave her a kiss. The spell was broken!

The princess opened her eyes and looked at
him.

"Is it you, my prince? I have waited such a
long time!" she said.

THE PRINCE, CHARMED BY THESE WORDS, LIFTED HER OFF THE BED. THE CASTLE WOKE.

THE COOK FINISHED ICING THE CAKE,

THE PAGE BOY ATE HIS CHOCOLATE,

THE MAID RAN AWAY FROM THE FOOTMAN,

THE DOG CHASED THE CAT,

THE BUTLER PUT THE GLASSES ON THE TABLE

AND THE LORDS AND LADIES WENT ON GETTING READY FOR THE PARTY.

The prince and princess talked for hours. The princess had so much to say after her long sleep. The prince told her that he loved her better than he loved himself and asked her to marry him. She had dreamt of him for a hundred years and she knew he was the prince of her dreams.

The king and queen were delighted to find their daughter in love with such a handsome prince. The cook was a bit muddled. Surely she was preparing for a birthday party, not a wedding?

"You are doing both, dear lady!" said the king. "But let us eat before we all die of hunger."

So the birthday party became a wedding feast which lasted for seven days and seven nights.

The prince and princess lived very happily. They had sixteen children and their favourite story was, of course, the story of Sleeping Beauty.

THE PRINCESS

ONCE UPON A TIME THERE LIVED A PRINCE WHO WISHED VERY MUCH TO MARRY A REAL PRINCESS. His search for a bride took him around the world and back again, which is a very long way indeed.

He met lots of girls who called themselves princesses: pretty ones, plain ones, vain ones, happy ones, sad ones and mad ones. But there was always something not quite right. It was a problem. How was he to know if they were real princesses?

AND THE PEA

At last he gave up and went home, feeling very upset. The king and queen agreed with their son. There was no point in marrying a girl who was not a real princess. What was to be done?

Then, one wild and stormy night, a princess was being driven home from a party when her car went too fast round a corner, and she was thrown into a ditch. The chauffeur did not see what had happened and drove on, leaving the princess all

a l o n e .

"WELL, THIS IS A PICKLE," SAID THE PRINCESS, PICKING HERSELF UP. "No point staying here. I'd better try and find some shelter."

She stumbled through the howling gale and pouring rain until she came to a palace.

"There must be someone here who can help me," the princess said to herself. So she rang the bell and was brought before the king and queen. She looked a terrible mess. Her hair was dripping wet, her dress was torn, her shoes were all muddy, and she had lost her crown.

The king and queen were surprised that this girl called herself a princess, but they were kind enough to invite her to stay. She could not very well go out again on a night like this.

After she had had a bath and been given some
clean clothes, the princess was brought to the
great hall for supper. The prince thought she
looked very nice, but what was the point of
falling in love when she might not
be a real princess at all?

   The queen had an idea.
"Too many girls these days,"
she said, "pretend to be
princesses. There is only one
way of knowing for certain if
this is a **real** princess."

61

S O THE QUEEN WENT INTO THE GIRL'S
BEDROOM AND PLACED ONE tiny PEA
UNDER THE MATTRESS. Then she ordered
twenty more mattresses to be put on top. She
was still not sure if there were enough
mattresses, so she ordered another twenty to be
put on top of them.

When the princess went to bed she needed a ladder to climb to the top of all those mattresses, but because she was a guest she couldn't very well ask why there were so many when just one would have done nicely.

The bed, for all its forty-one mattresses, was very uncomfortable. The princess was sure the mattresses were filled with rocks instead of feathers.

IN THE MORNING THE KING AND QUEEN ASKED HER HOW SHE HAD SLEPT.

"I couldn't sleep at all, your majesty," said the princess. "The bed was so lumpy and bumpy that I am bruised black and blue all over."

The king and queen were delighted. There could be no doubt that this was a real princess, for only a real princess is tender enough to feel one tiny pea through so many mattresses. The prince was keen to marry her. The princess was happy to marry him, too, for it is not easy to find a real prince these days. **Real** princes are quite rare.

You can see that this prince and princess were made for each other. In no time at all they were married, and they lived happily ever after. Now, isn't that a tender-hearted tale?

As for the pea, it was put in a museum, or was it the soup? Do you know? I quite forget.

SNOW

ONE SNOWY DAY LONG AGO, A QUEEN SAT BY HER WINDOW SEWING. While she stitched, her thoughts went to the baby she was going to have. Opening the window to feed her doves, she pricked her finger on her needle. Three drops of blood fell on to the snow. The queen looked at the redness of the blood, the whiteness of the snow, and the blackness of the ebony window frame and said to herself, "I wish my baby's skin to be as white as snow, her lips as red as blood and her hair as black as ebony."

Soon after this the queen gave birth to a beautiful little girl whom she named Snow White: but happiness turned to sorrow, for the young queen died. The king was mad with grief. He could not bring himself even to look at his little daughter. Snow White was taken away to be brought up in another part of the great palace, where her father could not see her.

A year passed and the king married again - not for love, but for land and riches. His new queen was very beautiful and very vain. Each day she would spend hours looking at herself in her magic mirror. Then she would ask,

"MIRROR, MIRROR ON THE WALL,
WHO IS THE FAIREST OF US ALL?"

and the mirror would answer,

"You, queen, are the fairest in the land."

For the queen could not bear to think that anyone was more beautiful than she was. What the mirror couldn't see was the queen's heart, which was ugly and cruel.

Seven years passed and Snow White grew up, long forgotten by her father and hidden from her stepmother the queen. Snow White grew more and more beautiful. Her skin was as white as snow, her lips as red as blood and her hair as black as ebony.

Then one day the queen asked the mirror her usual question and it answered,

"You, queen, may lovely be, it's true, but Snow White is far more beautiful than you."

When the queen heard this she turned pale with rage and envy. She called for her huntsman and told him: "I never want to see Snow White again. Take her away and kill her, and make sure you bring me her heart so that I know she's really dead."

The huntsman listened with great sadness. He took Snow White to the edge of a dark forest where bears lived and wolves howled at night, but he could not bring himself to harm this beautiful and gentle little girl.

"Run away from here, Snow White," said the huntsman. "Your stepmother the queen wants you dead."

Snow White was so frightened that she ran straight into the forest. The huntsman watched her go, feeling as if a great weight had been lifted from him. Then he killed a young deer and placed its heart in a box to give to the queen.

"I won't be lying when I say Snow White is dead," said the huntsman to himself, "for no one comes out of the dark forest alive."

As Snow White went further into the forest it grew darker and darker. The trees tangled together and all around her glinted the eyes of wild animals.

Snow White was scared. She stumbled and fell, and burst into tears. But picking herself up, she found to her surprise that she was standing on a path which led to the door of a little cottage.

"Perhaps there's someone here who can help me," she thought, and she pushed open the door. To her amazement the lights went on and the fire began to glow warmly. But the strange thing was, there was no one at home. The cottage was neat and tidy. In the middle of the room stood a long table covered with a green cloth. On it were laid seven little bowls and seven little glasses. Snow White sat down at the table and waited.

"Someone must live here," she thought, and as if by magic all the bowls were filled and wine poured into all the glasses. Snow White was quite amazed, but she was so hungry that she ate some food, which was delicious, and drank some wine.

Feeling very sleepy, she went upstairs.
There she found seven little beds, neatly made.
She hoped very much that no one would mind
if she lay down on one of the beds and had a
little rest, and soon she was fast asleep.

This little cottage hidden away in the heart of the forest belonged to seven dwarves, who had lived there for as long as anyone could remember. During the day they worked in their diamond mine, and at night they returned home to their cottage. All their spare time was spent inventing all kinds of wonderful machines to make their lives easier. Every night when they came home and opened the door, the lights would come on and the fire would start to burn. Their bowls would be filled with piping hot food and their glasses with home-made wine.

But tonight, when they saw their dear little cottage they froze, for the lights were already lit.

"It's a burglar," said the first dwarf.
"Don't be daft," said the second.
They all went closer and gingerly pushed
open the front door. All was as it should be
except that the food in the bowls was cold and
one bowl and one glass were empty.

"It must have been
someone," said the third
dwarf.

"Food doesn't
get eaten by itself,"
said the fourth dwarf.

"Perhaps it was a
bear," said the
fifth dwarf.

The sixth dwarf went upstairs and came rushing down again.

"There's a girl asleep in my bed!" he said.

"Then we'd better go and have a look," said the seventh.

In the morning Snow White woke to find seven faces staring down at her.

"Who are you?" they asked.

Snow White told them about her wicked stepmother and how the kindhearted huntsman had let her go. The seven dwarves had all heard of the cruel queen, and they were very worried.

"We can't just go off to work and leave Snow White on her own," said one of the dwarves.

"No!" said another dwarf. "The queen is bound to find out that she is still alive and to come searching for her."

"Yes!" said a third. "She is only little, like us, and we must look after her."

All that day the seven dwarves busied themselves inventing new things to keep Snow White safe.

They fitted an alarm bell between the cottage and the mine so that Snow White could warn them if she was in danger. They built a pretend bear to stand guard and growl if a stranger was about. And they made several traps in case the queen was foolish enough to come this way.

The next day the seven dwarves set off for
the mine. "Be careful, and whatever you do,
DON'T LET ANYONE INTO THE
COTTAGE," they told Snow White.

Meanwhile, the queen believed Snow White was dead, so she was content. Her magic mirror was silent. Then one day she could stand the mirror's silence no longer. She said,

"MIRROR, MIRROR ON THE WALL,
WHO IS THE LOVELIEST OF US ALL?"

The mirror answered,

"You, queen, may lovely be, it's true,
but the seven dwarves hide one more
beautiful than you."

When the queen heard this she was furious. The huntsman had betrayed her. She could not bear to think that there was anyone alive more beautiful than she was. She decided she must kill Snow White herself. She could trust no one else to do it. So she made two magic potions, one of them poisonous and the other for her disguise. She dipped a red apple in the poison and boiled the other magic potion until only a teaspoon of liquid remained. Then, staring into her magic mirror, she drank.

The queen began to shrivel and shrink, wrinkle and wither. Looking out at her from the mirror was the face of an ugly old woman. The mirror turned black and shattered into a thousand slivers of glass.

The queen laughed. "Even you, my magic mirror, can't recognise me now." From her secret box she took a magic cloak that would make her as invisible as night. She placed the poisoned apple in her basket and set off for the cottage where the seven dwarves lived.

Today Snow White was planning to make an apple pie. Although she was only seven years old, she was a very good cook and she loved to help the seven dwarves. It was growing cold and snow had started to fall. She had just rolled out the pastry when she heard the pretend bear growl a warning. Looking up, she saw an ugly old woman standing in the doorway.

"Hello, my dear," said the old woman. "I have the most delicious apples in my basket! Would you like one?"

"This old lady can't harm me," thought Snow White. "She doesn't look anything like the queen." So she let the old woman in.

"Do you live around here?" asked Snow White.

"No, my dear," said the queen. "I pass this way once a year and I always leave some apples for the little men."

"That's very kind of you," said Snow White.

The queen took the red apple from her basket and held it out for Snow White. "But this one is just for **you**," said the queen.

"Oh, it's so **red** and shiny!" said Snow White. She took one bite and fell down **dead**.

The alarm bell rang out in the mine. At once the dwarves dropped their tools and rushed towards the cottage. The queen, wrapped in her magic cloak, fled into the forest, but the cloak got caught in one of the traps and she was forced to leave it behind. Now she was invisible no longer. The dwarves were chasing after her, and in her panic she began to scramble up the slippery mountainside. A wolf howled and the queen missed her footing, fell and was smashed to smithereens on the rocks below.

When the seven dwarves found Snow White they were heartbroken. They laid her on a little bed and watched and wept over her for three days and three nights. They couldn't bring themselves to bury her in the cold ground, so they made a glass coffin, engraved on it the words,

HERE LIES SNOW WHITE
A KING'S DAUGHTER

and placed the glass coffin outside. They took it in turns to watch over her, and the birds and animals of the forest came to keep her company.

Ten years passed, but, strange as it may seem, Snow White kept growing, and by magic the tiny glass coffin grew with her.

Then, one day a prince came riding by.

He had dreamt that his heart belonged to a princess with skin as white as snow, lips as red as blood and hair as black as ebony. The moment he saw Snow White he knew he had found her.

The prince asked the dwarves to let him take the coffin back to his palace.

"I will pay you any amount of money," he pleaded.

"We will not part with her for all the gold in the world," said the seven dwarves. But they could see the prince truly loved Snow White, and at last they took pity on him and gave him her coffin.

The moment the coffin was moved, the piece of apple which had been stuck in her throat fell from her lips and Snow White woke up.

"Where am I?" she asked.

"You are safe with me," said the prince.
"I love you with all my heart." He knelt on
the ground and asked his beautiful princess to
marry him.

Snow White looked into the prince's eyes
and knew she loved him.

Snow White wanted the seven dwarves to be guests of honour at her wedding, for without them she would never have lived to meet her prince. So they all went back to the prince's palace together.

The wedding was magnificent, and it is true to say that Snow White and her prince …

lived happily ever after.

About the Stories

Everyone loves a princess, so it is not surprising that the stories in this book have been told in many ways and by many voices down the years. Their magic holds, because these fairy tales hide truths and secrets children recognize, and allow the listener to face the changes and challenges the princesses themselves live through.

Snow White and *The Frog Prince* were first written down by the Brothers Grimm, *Cinderella* and *Sleeping Beauty* by Charles Perrault, and *The Princess and the Pea* by Hans Andersen. These are the versions most of us know best, but the stories themselves are much, much older. Now I have told them in my own way, for the children of today.

Sally Gardner